MUSEUM *of* HIDDEN BEINGS

A Guide to Icelandic Creatures of Myth and Legend

Museum of Hidden Beings:
A Guide to Icelandic Creatures of Myth and Legend

Published by Eye of Newt Books Inc. • www.eyeofnewtpress.com
Eye of Newt Books Inc. 56 Edith Drive, Toronto, Ontario, M4R 1C3

First edition published by Salka, 2016;
Second edition printed by Eye of Newt Books Inc., 2021

ISBN: 9781777081713

Library and Archives Canada Cataloguing in Publication

Title: Museum of hidden beings : a guide to Icelandic creatures of myth and legend /
Arngrímur Sigurðsson.
Other titles: Dyldýrasafnið. English
Names: Arngrímur Sigurðsson, 1988- author.
Description: 2nd edition. | Series statement: Wool of bat | Includes bibliographical references.
Identifiers: Canadiana 20220169705 | ISBN 9781777081713 (softcover)
Subjects: LCSH: Animals, Mythical—Iceland. | LCSH: Animals—Folklore. | LCSH: Folklore—Iceland.
Classification: LCC GR825 .A7413 2022 | DDC 398.2094912/045—dc23

Printed in China

Arngrímur Sigurðsson

MUSEUM *of* HIDDEN BEINGS

A Guide to Icelandic Creatures of Myth and Legend

Belief in supernatural beings is a universal phenomenon. Every culture presents its own set of fantastical inventions. Over the course of eleven centuries, the people of Iceland have produced an abundance of these creatures. This compendium describes thirty-four of them in words and paint. The texts that accompany the paintings are drawn directly from Icelandic sagas and folklore, some of which have been translated for the first time. They present a unique insight into a different paradigm, where fantasy and imagination played a key part in human experience, a culture where monsters, elves, and trolls dominated the dark unknown, and where spells and sorcery shaped the world and the minds of ordinary people. This perspective may seem foreign to us in a time where the scientific mode of consciousness reigns supreme. However, experiences with these shadowy and elusive beings are still relatively common in the twenty-first century.

The origins of these stories can be traced back to the time when Norwegian exiles set sail in their longships to a far-flung and isolated island on the edge of the Arctic Circle to found a new independent nation. They named it Iceland. Barren and remote, it was the least likely of promised lands. The first settlers and the generations that came after them—Scandinavians, with a strong tradition of storytelling; along with settlers of Irish descent, who came from another of Europe's literary hotspots—joined forces in a creative outpouring that has few parallels in history.

In the centuries after settlement, a plethora of stories and poetry were written down on hundreds of cowhides. These writings are known as the sagas. They are expansive naturalistic narratives about real people that have captivated audiences for centuries and still enjoy attention to this day.

Not as well recognized, but no less remarkable, is the folklore. It is a complex oral heritage that, although frequently referred to in medieval sources, was not properly recorded until the nineteenth century, when a handful of scholars put it into writing under the helm of prolific collector and cultural researcher Jón Árnason.

These tales are interwoven into the fabric of the Icelandic literary tradition, containing numerous references and motifs from the mythology found in Snorri Sturluson's *Prose Edda*, as well as other sources such as the *Book of Settlements*, which records a multitude of place names across the country that refer to folklore and the imaginary creatures described therein. Elf hillocks, dwarf rocks, and nykur pits are numerous, and most of these places are associated with tales and legends about the beings that inhabit them.

The dark characters described in these stories are, however, not totally homespun. They have parallels in traditions as close as the British Isles and as far away as Saudi Arabia and Persia. The elves have their roots in the fairy faith of the British Isles, and the nykur, or water horse, has a kinsman in the German nix. The lyngbakur was described in Persian and Arabian sources as far back as the seventh century. Experiences with mermen and mermaids are reported in most seaside communities, and stories of ghosts and spirits are universal.

Supernatural experiences are still relatively common in Iceland. According to a recent report by a psychologist at the University of Iceland, Dr. Erlendur Haraldsson, animistic beliefs are widespread. Around 78 percent of Icelanders have experienced some form of paranormal phenomena, with 15 percent of men and 24 percent of women having experienced some kind of phenomenon described in folklore, with elves and spiritual companions being the most common. There are also recorded instances of the Icelandic Road Administration using public funds to pay mediums and clairvoyants to negotiate with local elf populations on worksites. This sometimes results in compromises, where elf hillocks are transported to new locations, though it can also lead to costly measures such as building roads around problematic areas instead of through them.

The hidden beings are indeed still with us, though immaterial and imaginary. My work aims to introduce them to a fresh audience through painting, and to pay homage to the anonymous authors who conjured up the unique tales that have inspired some of Europe's most cherished writers.

The artworks in this book are oil paintings that were painted between 2013 and 2016. Descriptions are taken verbatim from collections of folklore and old literature, with slight modifications to spelling and punctuation and abridged as necessary.

Reykjavík, April 2016

Arngrímur Sigurðsson

Table of Contents

Nissi

Dwarf Elf

A *nissi* is a dwarf elf, according to foreign folklore. They are wise, good-looking, somewhat reminiscent of light elves, and unlike common ghosts. They are benevolent, but playful and mischievous. They are short in stature, with particularly short legs, as is usual with dwarfs.

Seafarers generally believe in the existence of the nissi and tell tales of them. Icelandic seamen usually describe them as being the size of full-grown men, which is understandable as they tend not to distinguish between them and ship ghosts. Some describe these Icelandic nissi as being protectors of vessels and men, as is most often the case, despite their occasional mischievousness. Their protectiveness can also be construed as concern for their own well-being. They fear risking their life at sea and abandon doomed ships, as they can foretell their fate. [...] Regardless of whether the nissi are kin to fairies, elves, or ghosts, they are usually benevolent and joyful and friends to seafarers. They guide them in their fishing, warn them of impending dangers, and predict changes in the weather. Their merriment and laughter is a sign of an impending storm, its force in proportion to the intensity of the nissi's laughter. If they appear solemn and mournful, they predict misfortune or death on board. Their abandoning a ship, however, is a sure sign of the ship being doomed to destruction.

Sigfús Sigfússon, Íslenzkar þjóðsögur og sagnir III, p. 294.

Flæðarmús

Tide Mouse

The tide mouse mostly dwells on the ocean floor, preferably at great depths. It is shaped like a field mouse, only larger. The tide mouse needs silver (some say gold) in order to survive, and it only comes ashore if great tidings are foretold. Good fortune awaits those who succeed in capturing a tide mouse. They must immediately place it in a waterproof container, pour seawater over it, and put a silver (or gold) coin in the container. A day later, another coin of equal value will have appeared alongside it. The coin that was placed in the container is then removed, and this procedure is repeated once every day. One must also remember to change the creature's seawater daily.

Þorsteinn M. Jónsson, Gríma hin nýja III, p. 220.

Útburður

Spirit of an Abandoned Newborn

When mothers abandon their newborn children, leaving them where they will not be found, they turn into a ghost known as an *útburður*. When they are seen, their appearance resembles that of a bird, such as a raven. They raise themselves up on one knee and one hand and flutter about. Their colour depends on the colour of the rag in which they were wrapped. Those who see an útburður should not hesitate to follow it, as it will eventually flee to its mother. They howl intensely during bad weather but rarely speak. An exception to this is the tale of an útburður visiting its mother in a sheepfold and reciting the following verse to her:

My mother in the fold of sheep,
Do not worry, do not weep,
I shall lend you my blood-red rag
For you to wear, for you to wear.

Jón Árnason, Íslenzkar þjóðsögur og œvintýri III, p. 290.

Dvergur

Dwarf

Although the *Prose Edda* refers to dwarfs as being a kind of elf race, a clear distinction is made in folklore. Dwarfs appear in numerous adventures and chivalric tales. They are excellent craftsmen, dependable and loyal to their friends but extremely vengeful if crossed. Great benefits can be reaped from their friendship. They are mainly distinguished from true elves by their shape and build. They have very short legs, a bulky body, no beard, and a large head. They seem to manifest themselves as either human figures or spirits, and they always dwell in rocks. They do not have the physical strength of elves, humans, or trolls but compensate with their wisdom and craftsmanship. They avoid humans, and men must earn their friendship with gifts or persistence. There are few tales of dwarfs told in Iceland, so they must be few in number compared to other beings, such as elves and trolls.

Sigfús Sigfússon, Íslenzkar þjóðsögur og sagnir III, p. 186.

Hafstrambi

Sea Stack

It is reported that the monster called *hafstrambi* is found in the seas of Greenland. This monster is tall and of great size, and rises straight out of the water. It appears to have shoulders, neck and head, eyes and mouth, and nose and chin like those of a human being; but above the eyes and the eyebrows it looks more like a man with a peaked helmet on his head. It has shoulders like a man's, but no hands. Its body apparently grows narrower from the shoulders down, so that the lower down it has been observed, the more slender it has seemed to be. But no one has ever seen how the lower end is shaped, whether it terminates in a fin like a fish or is pointed like a pole.

No one has ever observed it closely enough to determine whether its body has scales like a fish or skin like a man. Whenever the monster has shown itself, men have always been sure that a storm would follow. They have also noted how it has turned when about to plunge into the waves and in what direction it has fallen. If it has turned toward the ship and has plunged in that direction, the sailors have felt sure that lives would be lost on that ship; but whenever it has turned away from the vessel and has plunged in that direction, they have felt confident that their lives would be spared, even though they should encounter rough waters and severe storms.

Konungs skuggsjá, p. 52–53. Written in the thirteenth century. Author unknown.

Finngálkn

Sphinx

Finngálkn is a creature mentioned in numerous ancient tales and legends, including the *Saga of Örvar-Oddr*, the *Saga of Hjalmther*, *Njal's Saga*, and many more. The descriptions therein depict them as large animals, extremely vicious and dangerous, sometimes carrying a sword in their claws. Occasionally they seem to be envisioned as coming from the sea. They are described as having the upper body of a human and the lower body of an animal. [...] More recent tales tell of their origin and claim a considerably less formidable size for them. (A finngálkn is, on occasion, said to be a sphinx.) According to later tales, the creature has a fox for a mother and a cat for a father, sometimes the other way around. Others say that roosters will sometimes lay eggs and that a finngálkn emerges when such an egg is hatched.

A finngálkn is wary of humans but dangerous to livestock. It is faster than any other animal, and no firearms can do it harm unless the sign of the cross is first made over the barrel and a silver button used for a bullet. A finngálkn is worse than any other creature sent to haunt the land of men. Icelandic annals tell of an incident in 1383 where a rooster laid an egg. In order to prevent the creature known as finngálkn from hatching from the egg, the rooster and its egg were burned. But when the egg burst open in the flames, observers noted that the hatchling seemed to be worm-shaped. A finngálkn has a deadly gaze.

Sigfús Sigfússon, Íslenzkar þjóðsögur og sagnir VI, p. 60–61.

Fylgja

Spirit Companion

Folklore claims that when a baby is born, part of its soul remains, as a unique being, in the membrane that surrounds it in the womb and which later emerges as the afterbirth. This being is called a *fylgja* and will become the baby's leader and, most likely, protector. It was referred to as sacred and may have been associated with destiny and fortune in previous times, sometimes to be bestowed upon friends and their kin.

As this was the case, good care was to be taken of the afterbirth. This did not prove to be easy, however. It was often cast out, sometimes to be devoured by scavengers or stepped on by men and animals. It was furthermore claimed that the fylgja would take the form of whoever first stepped over it or ate it. Prudent parents and attending women would thus bury it, preferably under a threshold or where the mother would pass first and most frequently, so that the fylgja would take her shape and be virtually indistinguishable from her appearance.

Because of the ever-present chance of men and animals preceding the mother, the custom of burning the afterbirth became common. This is said to be the reason why so many now have a fylgja in the shape of a gleam, glimmer, moon, or light, although they can allegedly take any form. People have now taken up the custom of using a light to make the sign of the cross over a newborn baby for this purpose.

Something or another accompanies each person, benevolent or malicious in nature. Some fylgjas are attached to abodes, and many are attached to various sites and domains. Land, air, fire, and water can also have fylgjas of their own.

Sigfús Sigfússon, Íslenzkar þjóðsögur og sagnir II, p. 283.

Fjörulabbi

Shore Laddie

Inhabitants of the West Fjords often catch sight of an animal emerging from the sea and onto the shore. Some believe it to be a sea otter, but the locals refer to it as a shore laddie. They say that its size and shape resembles that of sheep. The shore laddie is most often seen on land during the breeding season of the ewes, allegedly to serve as their ram. It is said that when ewes frequent shores where a shore laddie has been spotted, many deformed lambs, resembling the shore laddie in appearance are subsequently born. Many accounts support this, including this one:

One early winter evening in Bjarnarhöfn by Breiðafjörður, six men went out to see whether missing sheep had returned to the farm. They observed something moving by the shed and rushed to grab hold of the sheep and take it inside. When they came closer, they realised that this was no sheep. They formed a circle around the creature, which then took off towards the sea, pursued by the men, including my narrator. It ran as quickly as a dog and escaped into the ocean. It had a short, round head but otherwise resembled a dog rather than a sheep. It had a hump on its back and jumped frequently as it ran.

Sigfús Sigfússon, Íslenzkar þjóðsögur og sagnir V, p. 96.

Loftandi

Air Spirit

On a clear spring day, just after noon, a rumble was heard from the sky, similar to the sound of a large boat being dragged across gravel. This was heard widely across Suðurnes, in Keflavík, Grindavík, Garður, and Hafnarfjörður. In Miðnes, a cloud bank was observed at a spear's height above the horizon, drifting from the southeast to the south-west. It was dark at first but took on a pale pink hue as it approached the sun. According to the locals, the rumbling began when it had passed from view. When Kristinn Jakobeus heard of this, he remarked that his father had seen such a sight and that it had been called an air spirit.

Jón Árnason, Íslenzkar þjóðsögur og ævintýri IV, p. 27.

Sögusteinn

Tale Stone

Several accounts of tale stones exist. Ólafur of Purkey says that it can be found in the nest of the wagtail in May. It is to be kept in a bloody neck scarf and put in your right ear when you wish to learn something from it. It will then tell you everything that you might want to know.

Others describe the stone thus: When the first day of spring arrives during Holy Week, the raven will lay its eggs on Good Friday. One should approach the nest while Mass is being said. When the Passion is recited, the raven will lie on the eggs as if dead, and a stone will fall from its head and into the nest from where it can be retrieved. One should then harden it and carry it on one's person in a bag. When placed at the root of the tongue, one will be able to understand raven language.

A man who wants to acquire some knowledge is to tie the stone under his right armpit when he goes to bed and wrap his clothes tightly around his body. "Set your mind on that which you want to know before you fall asleep, and remember what you have learned when you awake."

One stone, grey in colour, can be found in sea foam. When placed in a lake, sediment appears, in which one can see one's face. "Then ask that which you want answered and be steadfast."

Jón Árnason, Íslenzkar þjóðsögur og ævintýri I, p. 649–650.

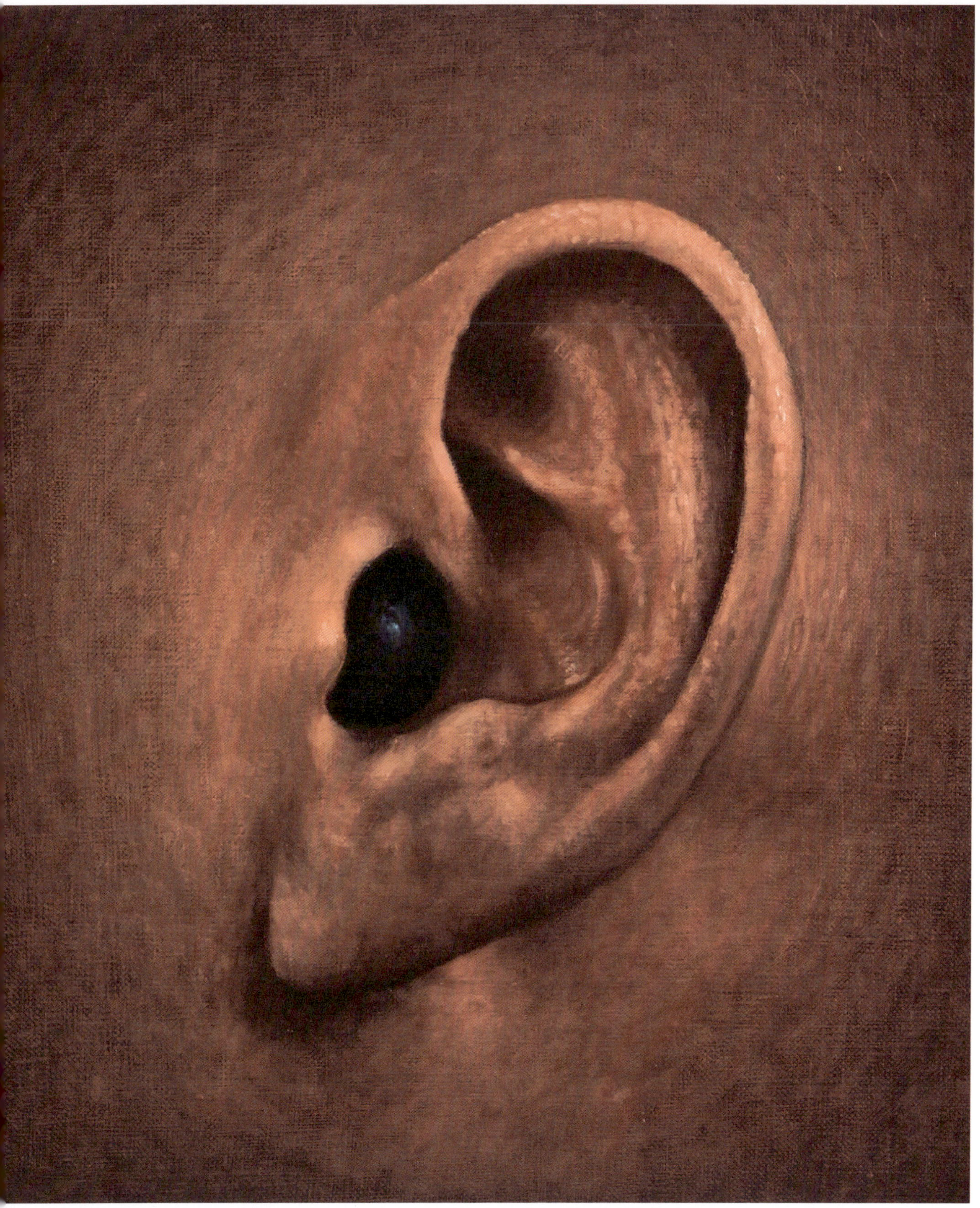

Sending

Sorcerer's Spectre

The fourth type of *sending*, and the most peculiar, consists of ghosts raised from natural substances by master sorcerers with comprehensive knowledge of life and matter. These men were supposed to be experts in the substances from which the bodies of men and animals are composed, their construction, and their structure. They are said to have made copies thereof, creating forms in which spirits could dwell. These allegedly had the appearance and substance of spectres, or even that of mist and vapour. The substances and their various compounds were stored in vials and had the appearance of a clear liquid. If ingested, they would cause insanity or dementia. If the liquid was poured out of the vial, it took the form of mist or a wisp of steam that could then be inhabited by any evil spirit that was present. If none was nearby, one could be conjured up. A few foreign apothecaries were said to possess these substances and dispense them in secret. Sorcerers would sometimes add substances to animal carcasses that they raised, thus endowing them with new qualities.

Sigfús Sigfússon, Íslenzkar þjóðsögur og sagnir III, p. 203.

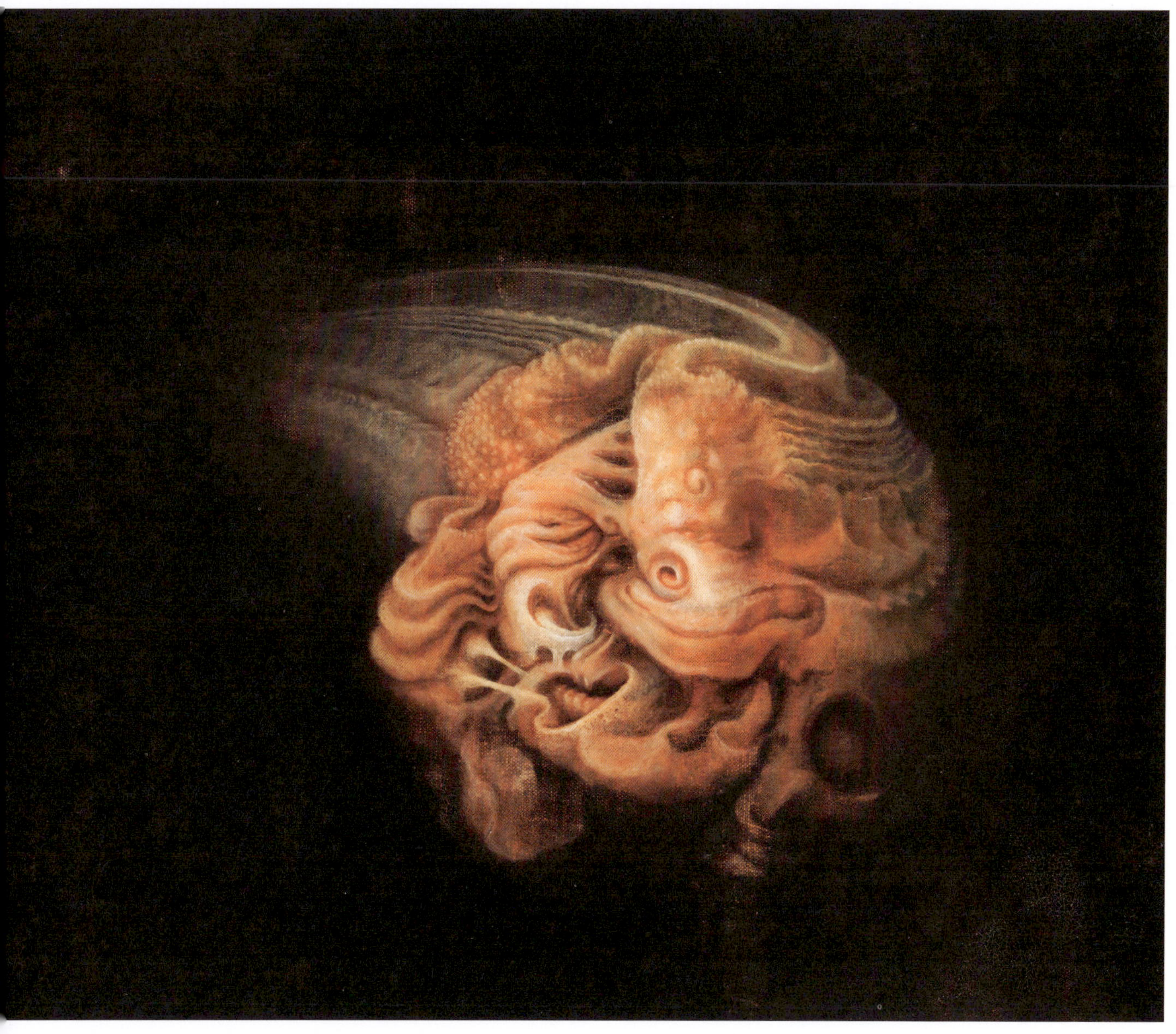

Dagtröll

Day Troll

Day trolls are trolls who walk abroad during bright days. They are fierce, but steadfast and loyal to their friends. Some are kinds of protective beings, often seeking to mate with humans but avoiding coming into conflict with them. They grant their descendants, the half-breeds, the hope of immortality. Day trolls have the gift of second sight and give good counsel to men. Some are malignant and cannibalistic. They have a human form but are usually unsightlier and much larger and more vicious in nature. They subsist by hunting and raising livestock and live in caves and behind waterfalls. This is why the cavities beneath waterfalls are known as a giant's kettle. Some tales of day trolls tell of friendship and loyalty, others of selfishness and violence, and others of fiendishness and atrocities.

Sigfús Sigfússon, Íslenzkar þjóðsögur og sagnir IV, p. 232–233.

Móri

Ghost

Shortly before the turn of the twentieth century, a young girl travelled from Reykjavík to the nearby hot springs of Laugar to do her washing. While at her work there, she felt an unpleasant presence and became sick at heart and nauseous. She looked around and was startled by the sight of a spectre or ghost crouching over a crock that stood on the ground close to her. Although frightened, she observed the sight before falling unconscious to the ground, where she lay until people came to look for her. When she came to, she told of what she had seen. It then came to light that the crock had contained human entrails. A doctor had dissected a corpse and wanted to have the entrails washed before inspection. The girl described the ghost in such vivid detail that the dead man could be recognized from her description. Few people knew of the presence of the entrails there. The source for this tale was an inhabitant of Reykjavík who was familiar with this matter.

Sigfús Sigfússon, Íslenzkar þjóðsögur og sagnir II, p. 27.

Tilberi

Milk Worm

A *snakkur*, or *tilberi*, is a creature that women create by first stealing a rib from a body that has recently been buried in a cemetery. On Whitsunday, they steal a piece of copper chipped from a church bell. They then pluck wool from between the shoulders of a newly shorn widow's sheep and wrap the wool around the human rib and piece of copper. They then keep the bundle between their breasts and spit wine on it when they take Communion, thus completing the creation of the tilberi. The tilberi must subsist by suckling on the woman herself. These women are easily recognizable as they walk with a limp and have a blood-red wart, resembling a teat, on the inside of their thigh, on which the tilberi suckles. A tilberi can be gotten rid of by making it gather and bring all sheep droppings from three highland pastures, as this will make it burst. In appearance, it is sausage shaped and bloated, curved at both ends, and very quick in movement.

Butter churned from milk stolen by a tilberi can be identified by making the sign of the cross in it, as it will then crumble into small pieces. This is why women make a cross with their finger in the butter when churning it. All butter handed in as payment to the dioceses carried this mark.

Jón Árnason, Íslenzkar þjóðsögur og ævintýri III, p. 453.

Kráki

Kraken

A fishing boat was sailing north of Iceland when it suddenly heeled, so that it was almost flooded, due to some horrific creature that held on to the gunwale. The part of it that was on board resembled some kind of pincers, but the head and body were outboard. The crew cleft the beast in twain at the gunwale. The part that fell on board was so large that they had to cut it up to get rid of it. They estimated that the whole creature must have been many shiploads.

Sigfús Sigfússon, Íslenzkar þjóðsögur og sagnir V, p. 125.

Moðormur

Worm Dog

A worm dog [...] is a female pup. The bitch will only give birth to one if it has consumed an unboiled cock egg. These have such an aberrant nature that the pup will become a monstrous creature [...] when it slips down into the earth on the third night after its birth and returns three years later as a monster with a deadly gaze. At birth, they will have an all-white or all-black body, a red head, and red feet. They are born with full sight.

María, wife of farmer Halli Snjólfsson at Sturluflötur in Fljótsdalur, was a labourer at the farm of Outer Víðivellir in her younger years. She later said that during her time there, an all-seeing, black female pup was born. Only its feet were red. It immediately stared at everything before it. The household did not want to risk having the creature nearby, so they placed it underwater in the hope that it would drown rather than slip into the earth. The creature was never seen again. At another farm, however, a one-coloured pup with a red head was born and managed to slip into the earth. A glass structure had to be built over the spot to prevent its return.

Sigfús Sigfússon, Íslenzkar þjóðsögur og sagnir VI, p. 63–64.

Hafmaður

Merman

It is rather common for seafarers to catch sight of both mermen and mermaids, and perhaps hafstrambis, as they raise their head and shoulders above the ocean and gaze for a moment at a vessel before diving back into the sea. Mermen are by far the most common of these sightings. All these sea creatures portend a storm, tempest, heavy seas, or loss of life in or by the sea.

A merman going up on dry land of his own accord carries the same portent. However, it is said that they are sometimes forced to go up on land while fleeing their enemies in the sea. In such cases, it is considered a great transgression and bad luck to harass them. They will sometimes flee from heavy waves onto quiet inlets or sand beaches, preferably in hard-to-reach places far from the dwellings of men. They will then rest there until they believe it safe to go back into the sea. In fact, they prefer being on land to being in the sea or fresh water, although it was said that it is usually their curiosity, importunity, and ferocity that makes them come on land. While on land, they would most often rest against a beach rock or stand up against a pillar or cliff, leaning on their elbow and with their paw resting against their cheek. Fierce mermen often try to drive men into the sea. Many have had to fight them with bludgeons. Some mermen are also said to be cannibals. [...] It is of no use to fire a gun at them except with silver buttons, as they shake off bullets and shells as if they were dust. Mermen most often come on land during the night. They avoid crowds, large ships, sharp noises and prolonged clatter. [...] Once in a while they would, for a lark, break into people's dwellings during the night and steal some item with which they would amuse themselves.

Sigfús Sigfússon, Íslenzkar þjóðsögur og sagnir V, p. 10–11.

Bezoar

Life Stone

Franciscan books tell of that most blessed and fortunate thing, the red bean, the "life stone" known as *bezoar.* The ancients wrote that it combines all benefits for life and health found in other natural stones, herbs, plants, and vines. It is called a life stone as it extends a man's life and gives him good health. The raven uses it to give its nestlings life, as the following account illustrates:

Sit down opposite a raven's nest and kill the nestling by strangling it. Place a small gag in its mouth so it appears to be half-open, then wait and observe. The raven will then, if it is able, fetch the life stone and place it in the nestling's mouth. As you see the nestling come alive, with the red stone in its mouth, you shall remove the stone and set the nestling free. The astute ravens vomit these good stones, hide them and keep careful watch over them. They are wise, cruel, and formidable.

Jón Árnason, Íslenzkar þjóðsögur og æventýri IV, p. 25.

Stökkull

Jumper

It is generally believed that the *stökkull* has flaps on its head that cover both eyes. It therefore cannot see anything in front of it unless it jumps out of the ocean. It is said that it jumps so high that not only does its whole body leave the water, but that both lowlands and smaller mountains can be seen under its tail, hence the name stökkull, or jumper. Jumping is the only way by which it can see what's in front of it, due to the flaps, and it travels a distance of four waves with each jump. To prevent it from being lured to the vessel, a stökkull is never to be called by its name at sea, as it is a vicious whale, eager to submerge anything that floats. As the stökkull jumps, it gazes around to see whether there is anything, a boat or something else, on which it can land. There are two ways to avoid being attacked by a stökkull. One is to throw a waterproof cask or buoy overboard for the stökkull to chase. It is said that the creature will exhaust itself by throwing itself repeatedly on it, as the cask or buoy will inevitably resurface. While this is going on, the boat will have plenty of time to escape. Another way to escape from an advancing stökkull is to steer the boat towards the sun, as the creature will not see the boat due to the glaring sun, even if it jumps.

Jón Árnason, Íslenzkar þjóðsögur og æventýri I, p. 626–627.

Ljósálfur

Light Elf

Elves are the noblest and most distinguished of all earthly creatures. Their similarity to us humans is such that when one hears of light elves, that most gentle breed of elves, one cannot help but think that they are our long-dead kinsmen and forefathers, reborn in this world on a higher plane of existence. Such is their resemblance to humans, yet they are more perfect. According to Snorri Sturluson's *Prose Edda*, the elves live in an abode in Heaven called Álfheimr:

There dwell the folk that are called light elves; but the dark elves dwell down in the earth, and they are unlike the light elves in appearance, but much more so in deeds.

Sigfús Sigfússon, Íslenzkar þjóðsögur og sagnir IV, p. 9.

Ormur

Giant Worm

It is said that a girl, who lived in either Hvammur or Dagverðarnes in Skorradalur, wanted to see whether it was true that placing a slug (lingworm) on a piece of gold would cause the slug, and the gold underneath it, to grow. She took a slug and placed it on a gold ring that she kept in her linen chest. But when she came back to look at the chest, it was close to bursting from the worm and gold within. The girl took fright and threw the chest and everything in it into the lake. The worm that grew on this girl's gold is the great worm that has occasionally been seen in Lake Skorradalsvatn.

Its size is so great that residents on the north side of Skorra-dalur have been able to see Dragafell, on the south side of the valley, under the worm's arch as it extends above the surface of the water, despite both its head and its tail being submerged. This has occurred only twice, once before the Black Death plague and once before the smallpox plague.

Jón Árnason, Íslenzkar þjóðsögur og æventýri IV, p. 15.

Sækýr

Sea Cow

There once was a man named Bjarni, known as Bjarni the Strong, who lived in Breiðavík by Borgarfjörður in the county of Múlasýsla. One summer day, Bjarni was out in the field in overcast and foggy weather when he heard the sound of cattle from the shore below the farm. He gazed into the fog and saw a herd of no fewer than eighteen cattle. A small boy ran behind the herd, followed by a calf. Bjarni took off and ran in front of the herd, as he suspected that these were sea cattle. When the boy saw this, he began egging the cattle on. Bjarni saw that first among the cattle was an ox with rings on its horns, which rattled as it ran. Bjarni and the boy raced until they came to the shore, by which time Bjarni had overtaken the calf. As the herd and the boy disappeared into the sea, Bjarni turned to the calf and burst the bladder between its nostrils, said to be present on all sea cattle, thus preventing it from returning to the sea. Bjarni then took it home. The calf, which was a heifer, became a fine cow from which a great breed descended in Breiðavík.

Jón Árnason, Íslenzkar þjóðsögur og ævintýri I, p. 129.

Skuggabaldur

Shadow Baldur

A *skuggabaldur* has a cat for a father and a fox for a mother. They are no less a menace than foxes or other beasts that sorcerers send to kill the livestock of others. Guns are of no use against them. One time, a skuggabaldur who had done much harm to sheep in the county of Húnavatnssýsla was cornered in a hole and killed by a flock of men. As it was stabbed, the skuggabaldur uttered: "Tell the cat at Bollastaðir that a skuggabaldur was stabbed today in the ravine." Those present found this highly peculiar. Later that day, the man who killed the skuggabaldur came to Bollastaðir to stay the night there. That evening, he recounted the tale as he lay on his bed. An old tomcat sat on a crossbeam. But when the man recited the words spoken by the skuggabaldur, the cat leaped on him and fastened its claws and teeth into his neck. The cat could not be removed until its head had been cut off, but by then the man was dead.

Jón Árnason, Íslenzkar þjóðsögur og æventýri I, p. 610.

Draumagras

Dream Weed

This plant is grey with a jointed stem and a bud on top. It grows earlier than any other plant and is fully grown by 16 May. It shall be plucked that day and kept in a Bible until the sixteenth Sunday after Trinity Sunday. It is to be finely chopped and mixed with Communion wine and ingested each morning on an empty stomach. This will stave off leprosy. If one takes a bite of it early in the morning while facing east, it will prevent all internal ailments. In that case, it shall also be plucked on that same day and kept in the same manner. If placed in one's hair before going to sleep, the dreamer will be made aware of that which he desires to know.

Jón Árnason, Íslenzkar þjóðsögur og œvintýri IV, p. 22.

Dökkálfur

Dark Elf

According to Snorri Sturluson's *Prose Edda*:

The light elves are fairer than the sun to look upon, but the dark elves are blacker than pitch.

The folklore does not make such a clear distinction, as the tales illustrate. Folk belief sometimes claims that these elves are descendants of the spirits cast down after the rebellion in Heaven. Jón Árnason describes the genesis of elves thus:

One day, God came to visit Adam and Eve. They greeted Him and showed Him all that they had in their abode. They also showed Him their children and He found them quite promising. He asked Eve whether they did not have any more children, to which she replied "no." In fact, she had not finished washing all her children and did not want God to see those who had not yet been washed. God knew this and replied: "That which shall be hidden from me shall also be hidden from men." Thus, these children became invisible to men and took refuge in hillocks and hills, knolls, and rocks. Elves are their descendants, while men are descended from the children that Eve showed to God. Elves are never visible to humans unless they choose so, as they can see humans and enable humans to see them in return.

Sigfús Sigfússon, Íslenzkar þjóðsögur og sagnir IV, p. 9.
Jón Árnason, Íslenzkar þjóðsögur og ævintýri I, p. 7.

Urðarköttur

Ghoul Cat

The *Urdarköttur* is in most respects like other cats [...] but larger and more vicious and formidable. As a youngling, it will bury itself into the ground, preferably in a cemetery, and stay there for an undetermined time. It will spare nothing once it has emerged and is almost impossible to conquer. It can grow to the size of a dog, wether, or even a yearling. It is said that when it buries itself in a cemetery and is left undisturbed, it will stay underground for three years, in which case it is known as a corpse cat. Once it leaves the cemetery, according to some accounts, it will dwell in rocky slopes, attacking sheep, birds, and men alike. Its gaze is so evil and severe that it proves instantly fatal to all beings, although this is mostly to be feared [...] when it is newly emerged from the ground. It is like other cats in that it will be overcome by its own reflection. I have heard few tales of actual ghoul cats. No guns will harm a ghoul cat with full powers, except perhaps if silver buttons or bullets are fired at it. These are among the worst of all malignant creatures.

Sigfús Sigfússon, Íslenzkar þjóðsögur og sagnir VI, p. 64–65.

Nykur

Water Horse

A *nykur* is a creature found in rivers and lakes and even the sea. It is similar to a horse in shape, usually grey but sometimes brown. Its hooves are turned backwards, and the fetlocks are reversed compared to other horses. These attributes are not constant, however, and the nykur can shift shapes suddenly and at will. A great rumbling can often be heard when ice cracks on winter days. This is said to be a nykur neighing. Its foaling is similar to that of horses, except it takes place underwater. A nykur will occasionally breed with horses. All horses sired by a nykur lie down when crossing belly-deep water, whether they are being ridden or carrying baggage. This is a trait inherited from the nykur, who will wait by difficult-to-cross rivers and lakes, acting tame and tempting men to ride it across. Once a man is on its back, it runs into the water and lies down, dragging the rider down into the water with it. A nykur cannot stand the sound of its own name, or any other word that sounds like it, and will run straight into the water upon hearing it.

Jón Árnason, Íslenzkar þjóðsögur og ævintýri I, p. 129–130.

Lyngbakur

Heather Back

Ancient tales tell of a whale monster, known as *lyngbakur*, that has the appearance of an island covered with a growth of heather. Lyngbakur is the second largest of all sea creatures, its size only exceeded by the *hafgúfa*. Örvar-Oddr and Vignir encountered a lyngbakur during their search for Ögmundr, killer of Eyþjófr. Their men believed it to be an island covered with heather, and several of them attempted to explore its surface, despite the warnings of Örvar-Oddr and Vignir. The creature then disappeared into the sea, taking all the men with it.

Few tales of the lyngbakur have been told in Iceland in recent times. An exception is the tale of brother and sister Magnús and Brandþrúður, children of "Cleft Palate" Benóný of Glettinganes in the county of Múlasýsla, both of whom were considered upright and honest. One spring as they were out fishing, they let their boat drift south along the peninsula, Brandþrúður holding the fishing line. As they came closer to the tidal race, they saw a large creature protruding from the water surface. It was shaped like a jellyfish and the size of a small islet or island. Its upper half resembled earth covered with heather. They had ventured close to it when they realized that the creature extended further below the surface, so they hurried back and away from it. Some believe that what they encountered was a lyngbakur.

Sigfús Sigfússon, Íslenzkar þjóðsögur og sagnir V, p. 139–140.

Martröll

Sea Troll

Sigtryggur left Húsavík late one night, as was his wont, and went his usual way along the shore. When he reached the Haukamýrdalur brook, close to Kaldbakur, he saw a creature approaching him from the sea. It appeared to have a human shape, but was rather larger than a man. He did not expect to see any people there and suspected, although it was dark, that the creature was not of this world. He turned and headed towards the turf, where there was a pile of wood from which he grabbed a stick that he felt could be used for a weapon. Just as he did so, the creature assailed him. They struggled violently, Sigtryggur beating the creature with his stick and the creature attacking him with full force. It seemed to Sigtryggur that the creature had arms, which it used to deliver many heavy blows. He felt no weakening of its strength or resolve, however hard he hit it. He began to lose courage, due to his increasing weariness and the many heavy blows he continued to receive. He eventually managed to land a blow on one of the creature's arms, at which it retreated and headed towards the sea. He was certain that he had broken the arm, as he saw it flail about when the creature turned back. He believed this to be the only reason for its retreat. Sigtryggur hurried from the shore and headed home, bearing the marks of the struggle described above.

No one who knew Sigtryggur doubts the truthfulness of this account.

Oddur Björnsson, Þjóðtrú og þjóðsagnir, p. 145–148.

Tröllbotnaland

Land of Giants

Tales tell of a country northeast of Iceland and Greenland known as the Land of Giants. Many have paid dearly for attempting to explore the land and its people, including Gorm the Old, King of Denmark, whose mission was hindered by heavy rain, raging storms, and other obstacles. Later, Harald Hardrada embarked on an expedition to the land but had to deal with dangers, deceptions, and darkness on the way before sailing his ship into a peculiar whirlpool, or vortex. He barely escaped and never reached the habitat of the giants. Many mocked Harald for his failure and presumed disappointment, and because of this, men from Norway and Friesland mounted another expedition to search for the Land of Giants. Their luck was not much better, as they endured countless unspeakable punishments meted out by Heaven, earth, and sea. They also sailed into the giant vortex, losing all sight of the sun during the ordeal.

They finally landed on the shore of the land and were met with high mountains and awesome cliffs. There were no houses or constructs to be seen, but many caves and holes had been dug into the earth. The ground was covered with gold and silver, which the crewmen began collecting and taking to their ship. The natives saw this and descended upon them, armed with spears and bows. The crew succeeded in escaping, except for one man who was left behind by accident and promptly torn limb from limb in the most horrific manner. It is said that bright daylight is never seen in this land and that a great rumbling is constantly heard from the sky and sea.

Gísli Oddsson, Annalium in Islandia Farrago, p. 12–13, written in 1637.

Nátttröll

Night Troll

The main distinction of night trolls is that they cannot stand to see sun or daylight, as this will turn them into stone. This makes them understandably wary of the light. They love the darkness and travel mostly by night, so they are less frequently seen than other trolls. They are ogres and cannibals, usually even larger, stronger, and more monstrous than other trolls. There are few accounts of their interactions with men, and their physical form sets them apart from all except the most fearsome monsters; those who swim around in the ocean or attempt to swim between countries, throw large rocks across great distances, stomp around cliffs, and cross whole valleys in a single step. But despite their size and might, night trolls have had reason to feel threatened by men, despite the difference in stature, and by nature itself, particularly the sun, which seems to be hostile to them and is likely to destroy them all in the end. Reminders of their fate at the hands of this giver of light and life are a common sight: petrified trolls, scattered about, awaiting Judgement Day. For they are the rock pillars so common in all mountains (particularly in the West and East Fjords). They never move, except perhaps in darkness and fog. Accounts of them all tell the same tale of aggression and cruelty, seldom affability.

Sigfús Sigfússon, Íslenzkar þjóðsögur og sagnir IV, p. 267–268.

Skeljaskrímsli

Shell Monster

Hallgrímur the Strong lived at Vík in Flateyjardalur in the early 1800s. Grímur was his son. One moonlit winter night, Grímur was lying in wait by the sea, hunting for foxes, when he saw a large and unfamiliar creature come on land. Its body gleamed like the skin of a whale and made a rustling sound like seashells rattling. The creature headed straight towards Grímur. When it had almost reached him, Grímur aimed the gun at its head and fired. Blood poured from the wound and the creature retreated back into the sea, never to be seen again. Gísli Jónasson of Svínarnes recounted this event, as told to him by Grímur himself. Gísli maintained that Grímur was a truthful and honest man.

Þorsteinn M. Jónsson, Gríma hin nýja III, p. 212.

Marbendill

Seaman

A *marbendill* lives on the ocean floor and is never seen above the surface unless caught by fishermen, as shall be recounted presently. The scabrous, cream-coloured limestone *Millepora polymorpha*, which is found on the ocean floor and often washes up on shore, is said to be the handiwork of a marbendill. The belief in these creatures is an old one, as evidenced by the *Book of Settlements* and the *Saga of Half and his Heroes*. Men have quite often caught a marbendill, usually by capturing it alive and hauling it onto their boat. Some of these were carrying fishhooks and a fishing net. There are also tales of them having been found dead, cast up on the shore or in the belly of a shark. When caught alive, they will try to escape back to their realm. They are taciturn and have little fondness for men.

Jón Árnason, Íslenzkar þjóðsögur og ævintýri I, p. 125–126.

Sálir

Souls

Dark are the murky waters,
The deep and stormy sea
Where each and every evening
This fisherman will be.
—Dark are the murky waters.

The first time that he cast
His fishhook overboard,
An old and splendid codfish
Became his sweet reward.
He mumbled something to himself
And sang and laughed and roared.

On every night since then
The man will go back there
And spend the evening fishing
With no need to despair,
For his boat is always full of catch
Though black storms shake the air.

Dark are the murky waters,
The deep and stormy sea,
And some say that the old man
Who rows there frequently
Has horns, a tail and claws
And a hoof below his knee.

When we die, the tale tells,
And death comes to your door,
The soul becomes a codfish
To cleanse what's gone before ...
And let's not say any more.
—But dark are the murky waters.

David Stefansonn, "Dark Are the Murky Waters," pp. 349–350.

The Dark Corners of the Mind

Iceland is, famously, a country of extremes.

The turbulent, often violent weather is a dominant force and a constant source of conversation in Icelandic life. A bad winter can whip the coastal towns and villages for months, throwing down torrential downpours of rain, metre-thick blankets of snow, sheets of blinding sleet, and gales that shake the windows. Leaving the house can become impossible—the weather sits over the country like a tangibly malevolent force, uncompromisingly dictating the rhythm of day-to-day life. So it's perhaps unsurprising that the centuries-old, ever-expanding coterie of Iceland's mythology comprises a cast of dark, mysterious spirits, fauna, and apparitions who spring forth from the elements.

Perhaps not coincidentally, some of these creatures act as cautionary tales. The sea-dwelling horse that leaps from the rough tide to pull in passersby also tells us not to walk too close to the violent surf. The living sea stack that towers over the shore rains down rocks to sink passing boats, and the story reminds careless sailors to take a wide berth. The lake monster whose imminent appearance cracks the frozen ice signals to reckless wanderers that it's time to head back to more solid ground.

Others seek to explain unwanted events by scapegoating alleged sorcerers. Conjuring the tilberi, a large worm that drains animals of milk and brings it back to its owner, was illegal in Icelandic law in the sixteenth century.

This sorcerous crime carried real-world ramifications according to historical accounts, at least one witch was burned at the stake for it. Others still are just plain bizarre, like Frísland—a phantom island roughly the size of Iceland that appeared on early maps for 100 years, before abruptly vanishing from history without a trace.

In the age of streetlights, rescue services, radiators, and Netflix, it feels easier to hold nature—and, by extension, its hidden beings—at arm's length. But it's different to read these pages while thinking about people huddled around a flickering fire in an old-fashioned, dirt-floored turf house, with the wind coming in through the walls, knitting, dreaming, and telling stories, for weeks or even months on end. It's easy to see how the impenetrable darkness, vicious storms, crashing tide, and gnarled lava were anthropomorphized, taking on tangible personalities of their own.

These creatures and legends have fired the imaginations of Icelanders for centuries, each one gaining strength and longevity with every retelling. *Museum of Hidden Beings* is an act of artistic cryptozoology that opens the door for creatures perhaps nearing extinction to thrive once more, travelling far outside of Iceland's black shoreline and finding new life in the minds of its readers.

John Rogers

Bibliography

Davíð Stefánsson. "Á Dökkumiðum," *Iðunn*, 1916–1917, p. 349–350.

Gísli Oddsson. *Íslensk annálabrot (Annalium in Islandia Farrago); Undur Íslands (De mirabilius Islandiœ)*, trans. Jónas Rafnar, Akureyri, Þorsteinn M. Jónsson, 1942.

Jón Árnason. *Íslenzkar þjóðsögur og œvintýri I–IV*, Reykjavík, Þjóðsaga, 1954–1961.

Konungs skuggsjá (Speculum Regale), Reykjavík, H.F. Leiftur, 1955.

Oddur Björnsson. *Þjóðtrú og þjóðsagnir*, Akureyri, Bókaforlag Odds Björnssonar, 1908.

Sigfús Sigfússon. *Íslenzkar þjóðsögur og sagnir*, Reykjavík, Víkingsútgáfan, 1922–1958.

Sigfús Sigfússon. *Íslenzkar þjóðsögur og sagnir*, 2nd edition, Reykjavík, Þjóðsaga, 1982–1993.

Þorsteinn M. Jónsson. *Gríma hin nýja*, Reykjavík, Þjóðsaga, 1964–1965.

About the Author

Arngrímur Sigurðsson (born 1988 in Reykjavík) is an Icelandic artist.

He trained as a painter at the Iceland Academy of the Arts and at the Academy of Fine Arts in Vienna. He published *Duldýrasafnið*, the Icelandic edition of the *Museum of Hidden Beings* in late 2014, and has since been involved with a number of commissions, collaborative projects, and exhibitions in Iceland and abroad.